Disney
Tangled

Autumn
Publishing

Once upon a time, in a land far away, an old woman named Mother Gothel possessed a magical golden flower. She hoarded its power to preserve her youth and beauty.

Centuries later, in a glorious kingdom, the beloved queen fell ill. The townspeople searched for the legendary flower, until at last they found it. The flower made the queen well, and she soon gave birth to a beautiful baby girl. The king and queen launched a lantern into the sky in celebration.

One night, the vengeful Mother Gothel slipped into the nursery, where she discovered that the healing power of the flower had transferred into the baby's golden hair!

Mother Gothel cut off a lock, but the hair lost its power and turned brown. So, she snatched the princess and vanished. The king and queen were heartbroken.

Each year on the princess's birthday, the king and queen released lanterns into the night sky, hoping their light would guide their princess home.

Mother Gothel kept Rapunzel locked in a tower and pretended to love her, although she only truly loved Rapunzel's golden hair.

On the day before her eighteenth birthday, Rapunzel told Mother Gothel something she'd dreamt of for years. "I want to see the floating lights!" she said. "They appear every year on my birthday – only on my birthday. And I can't help but feel like they're meant for me!"

Mother Gothel told Rapunzel she was too weak and helpless to handle the outside world.

Meanwhile, in another part of the forest, a thief named Flynn Rider was on the run with his partners in crime, the Stabbington Brothers. Flynn clutched tightly to a satchel that held a stolen royal crown!

Knowing the Stabbingtons were untrustworthy, Flynn took off with the satchel. But the Captain of the Guard and his horse, Maximus, were on his heels! Knocking the captain off Maximus, Flynn landed in the saddle himself and as Flynn yanked the satchel free from the horse's teeth, it went flying into the air.

The satchel snagged on a tree that extended over a cliff. Flynn and Maximus both made their way out onto the tree trunk. But the tree broke, sending the thief and horse toppling into the canyon below.

When they landed, Flynn took off before Maximus could pick up his scent.

Then, he came across an enormous tower. It was the perfect hiding place!

He climbed the tower and scrambled into the open window at the top.

Finally, he breathed a sigh of relief. He was safe!

CLANG!

Suddenly, everything went black.

Rapunzel had been so startled by the intruder, she sneaked up behind him and hit him with a frying pan!

The man didn't look like the scary ruffians that Mother Gothel had warned her about.

Rapunzel dragged Flynn to the wardrobe and stuffed him inside. Surely this act of bravery would prove to Mother that she could handle herself in the outside world.

Then, Rapunzel noticed the mysterious gold object in Flynn's satchel. She placed it on top of her head and gazed into the mirror. She felt different somehow.

Suddenly, Mother Gothel
arrived. Rapunzel brought up the
floating lights again.

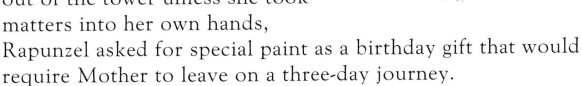

"We're done talking about this.
You are not leaving this tower!
EVER!" roared Mother Gothel.
Realising she would never get
out of the tower unless she took
matters into her own hands,
Rapunzel asked for special paint as a birthday gift that would
require Mother to leave on a three-day journey.

Mother Gothel agreed and left the tower. Rapunzel dragged
Flynn out of the wardrobe
and offered him a deal.
If Flynn took her to
see the floating
lights and
returned her
home safely,
she would
give him the
satchel. Flynn
had no choice
but to agree.

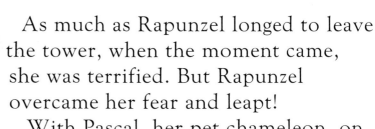

As much as Rapunzel longed to leave the tower, when the moment came, she was terrified. But Rapunzel overcame her fear and leapt!

With Pascal, her pet chameleon, on her shoulder, she slid down her hair, stopping just inches above the ground.

Slowly, Rapunzel touched one foot to the soft grass, then the other. "I can't believe I did this! she shouted, as she rolled on the ground.

Rapunzel was having the time of her life, but she also felt like a terrible daughter. One moment she was running gleefully through a meadow, the next she was sobbing facedown in a field of flowers.

Flynn tried to take advantage of Rapunzel's guilt by making her feel even worse. "Does your mother deserve this?" he asked. But Flynn's charms didn't work on Rapunzel.

"I'm seeing those lanterns," she insisted.

Not far from the tower, Mother Gothel saw Maximus.
"A palace horse," she gasped, seeing the kingdom's sun symbol on Maximus' chest. She thought the guards had found Rapunzel. She turned and frantically raced back to the tower.

Mother Gothel quickly realised Rapunzel was gone. Then, she saw the crown in the satchel, along with Flynn's WANTED poster. Now she knew exactly who had taken Rapunzel – and nothing was going to stop her from finding him.

Meanwhile, Flynn led Rapunzel to a pub called the Snuggly Duckling. Inside, the place was filled with scary-looking thugs and when someone held up Flynn's WANTED poster, people began fighting for the reward money.

Rapunzel banged her frying pan on a giant pot to get the thugs' attention. She asked them to let Flynn go so that she could make her dream come true. To Rapunzel's surprise, every one of the thugs had a secret dream too.

Outside, Mother Gothel arrived at the pub. She looked into the window and was shocked to see that Rapunzel had managed to befriend a room full of ruffians!

Suddenly, Maximus, the royal guards and the captive Stabbington Brothers burst into the pub.

One of the thugs revealed a secret passageway to Flynn and Rapunzel. They gratefully disappeared into the dark tunnel.

Moments later, Maximus led the guards straight to the escape route. However, the Stabbingtons headed down the passageway themselves. They wanted the crown back!

Mother Gothel had seen everything and made one of the thugs tell her where the tunnel ended.

Flynn and Rapunzel sprinted through the tunnel and skidded to the edge of an enormous cavern. Rapunzel lassoed her hair around a rock and they swung right over the Stabbington Brothers!

But suddenly a dam burst, filling the entire cavern with water! Maximus, the guards and the Stabbingtons were washed away, leaving Flynn and Rapunzel trapped. The water began to rise. As Flynn frantically searched for a way out, he cut his hand on the rocks.

"I'm so sorry, Flynn," Rapunzel said, tearfully.

"Eugene. My real name's Eugene Fitzherbert," Flynn admitted.

Rapunzel revealed a secret of her own: "I have magic hair that glows when I sing." Suddenly, she realised her hair could light up the cave and show them the way out.

At the tunnel's exit, Mother Gothel waited for Flynn and Rapunzel, but the Stabbington Brothers emerged instead. She offered them revenge on Flynn – and something even more valuable than the crown!

Meanwhile, Rapunzel, Flynn and Pascal had made it safely to shore. Rapunzel wrapped her hair around Flynn's injured hand and began to sing. Her glowing hair healed Flynn's wound.

He was finally beginning to understand how special Rapunzel was. When Flynn went to gather firewood, Mother Gothel appeared to take Rapunzel back to the tower.

But Rapunzel refused to go back. "I met someone, and I think he likes me," she said.

Mother Gothel laughed at her. She handed Rapunzel the satchel with the crown and told her that it was all Flynn wanted. Once Rapunzel gave it to him, the thief would vanish.

After Mother Gothel set the seeds of doubt, she retreated back into the forest. Rapunzel wanted to trust Flynn, but she wasn't sure. She decided to hide the satchel in a nearby tree.

The next morning, Flynn woke up to Maximus trying to drag him away. Rapunzel came to Flynn's rescue and talked the horse into letting the thief go free for one more day.

Suddenly, the entire kingdom came into view and Rapunzel gasped. Her dream was just hours away from coming true!

Rapunzel, Flynn, Maximus and Pascal entered the gates of the kingdom. The town was the most exciting thing Rapunzel had ever experienced. A little boy greeted Rapunzel with a kingdom flag that had a golden sun symbol on it. Then, a group of little girls braided Rapunzel's locks and pinned them up with flowers. Afterwards, Rapunzel and Flynn joined a crowd as a dance was about to begin.

Rapunzel was transfixed by a mosaic behind the stage. It was of the king and queen holding a baby girl with striking green eyes, just like her own.

"Let the dance begin!" called an announcer.

Rapunzel and Flynn joined hands and began to whirl around the square.

After they danced, the couple visited shops and enjoyed the sights. All the while, they were getting to know each other better. It was a wonderful day!

As evening approached, Flynn led Rapunzel to a boat and rowed them to a spot with a perfect view of the kingdom.

As lanterns filled the sky, Rapunzel's heart soared. She gave Flynn the satchel, which she had kept hidden all day. She was no longer afraid he would leave her once he had the crown.

Beneath the glow of the lanterns, Rapunzel and Flynn held hands and gazed into each other's eyes.

Then, Flynn spotted the Stabbington Brothers watching them. Quickly, he rowed the boat to land. "I'll be right back," he told Rapunzel, as he grabbed the satchel and strode off.

Flynn gave the brothers the crown, but they wanted Rapunzel and her magic hair instead! The brothers knocked Flynn unconscious, tied him to the helm of a boat and sent him sailing into the harbour.

The brothers told Rapunzel that Flynn had traded her for the crown. Rapunzel saw Flynn sailing away. She thought he had betrayed her! Rapunzel ran off into the forest, with the brothers in pursuit. Moments later, she heard Mother Gothel's voice. She ran back and found Mother standing over the unconscious Stabbingtons.

"You were right, Mother," said Rapunzel, tearfully.

Later, guards found Flynn with the stolen crown and arrested him. Maximus saw everything and knew he had to do something.

In prison, Flynn spotted the Stabbington brothers in a cell. They admitted that Mother Gothel had told them about Rapunzel's hair and double-crossed them.

Suddenly, the pub thugs from the Snuggly Duckling arrived and broke Flynn out of prison! They launched him over the prison walls and onto Maximus' back. Maximus had planned the entire escape! Flynn thanked him and, together, the heroes galloped off to rescue Rapunzel.

Back at the tower, Rapunzel was heartbroken. She held up the kingdom flag with the sun symbol and noticed she had been painting the sun symbol her whole life. She suddenly realised that she was the lost princess! Rapunzel tried to leave the tower, but Mother Gothel overpowered her. Flynn finally arrived at the tower. "Rapunzel! Rapunzel, let down your hair!" he called.

Rapunzel's golden locks fell to the ground and Flynn began to climb. When he reached the top, he found Rapunzel chained up. He went to help her, but Mother Gothel wounded him with a dagger.

Rapunzel begged Mother Gothel to allow her to heal Flynn. In return, Rapunzel promised she would stay with her forever. Mother Gothel agreed and unchained Rapunzel. She knew Rapunzel never broke a promise.

Rapunzel rushed to Flynn and placed her hair over his wound.

Suddenly, Flynn reached for a shard of broken glass and cut off Rapunzel's hair! It instantly turned brown and lost its magic healing power.

"What have you done?!" Mother Gothel cried. Within moments she aged hundreds of years and turned to dust.

Rapunzel cradled Flynn and a single golden tear fell upon his cheek. Flynn's entire body suddenly began to glow.

He was healed!

Flynn, Pascal and Maximus took Rapunzel straight
to the castle. Her parents were filled with joy. Their
daughter had finally been returned to them! Rapunzel felt
her parents' love surround her as they hugged each other
tightly.

Soon, all of the townspeople gathered for a welcome
home party. Floating lanterns were released into the sky.
Their light had guided the princess home at last.